# By the
# Light of the Moon

Written by Keith Faulkner
Illustrated by Jonathan Lambert

BARNES
&NOBLE
BOOKS
NEW YORK

The sun goes down, the moon is bright. It's time for creatures of the night.

The ghost is brushing her golden hair.
So she looks good when she's out to scare.

Skeleton pours cereal in his plate.
He really ought to gain some weight.

The witch is having her evening shower. She's due out spooking in half an hour.
The moon's just come up for the night. Looks like he's had a nasty fright.

The three friends meet upon the hill.    Their night's work is ahead.

They hurry down into the town to scare the folks in bed.

Into an open window, the witch begins to creep.

The ghost just passes through the wall and makes a dreadful wail.

Skeleton is in the dark, he then turns on the light.

She casts a spell, one she does well, on those who lie asleep.

If she could not detach her head, she couldn't tell this tale.

He finds he's in the dog pound and he gets a dreadful fright.

The people of the little town by now are wide awake.
After all the frights they've had it's more than      they can take.

They chase witch, ghost and skeleton both up the street and down.
They leap aboard the witch's broom - It's time that they left town.

The moon sinks down behind the hills. The sun will soon be bright.

The three friends hurry home, because they've spooked enough tonight.

The ghost is reading her book in bed.
Up in front of her disembodied head.

Skeleton always cleans his teeth each day,
But he does it in an very unusual way.

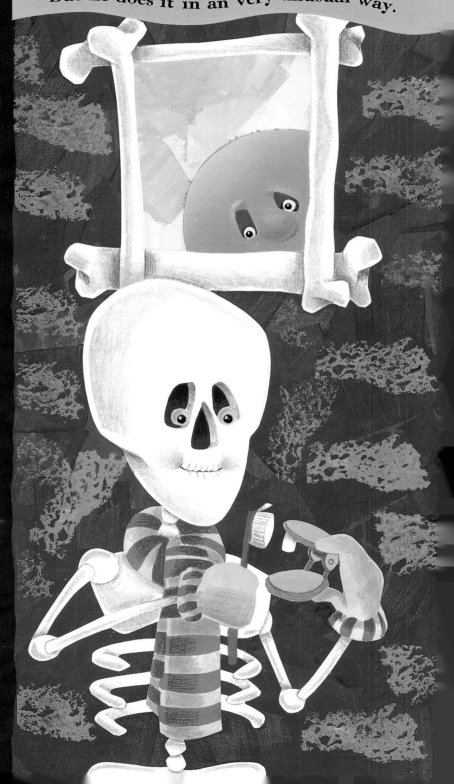